This guide is dedicated to all the dreamers and doers out there who have a passion for cosmetics and are looking to turn their dreams into reality. Whether you are just starting out or have been in the industry for a while, we hope that this guide will provide you with the tools, resources, and knowledge you need to successfully launch your own cosmetics brand.

To the beauty enthusiasts who are always on the lookout for the latest products, shades, and trends, thank you for your constant inspiration. Your unwavering support and love for cosmetics drives us to create this guide to help others follow their dreams.

To the entrepreneurs who have taken the leap of faith and launched their own cosmetics brands, thank you for your bravery and determination. Your stories of success and failure have provided us with valuable lessons that we have included in this guide to help others navigate the journey of launching a cosmetics brand.

And to all the makeup artists, skincare specialists, and beauty experts, thank you for sharing your skills, knowledge, and creativity with the world. Your passion for beauty has brought us all together, and we hope that this guide will help others follow in your footsteps.

We hope that this guide will be a valuable resource for you and that it will help you achieve your dream of launching a successful cosmetics brand. So let's get started!

COSMETICS BRAND LAUNCH: A COMPREHENSIVE GUIDE

TUSHAR RAJ

Made with ❤ on the Notion Press Platform
www.notionpress.com

Contents

Foreword

Starting your own cosmetics brand can be a thrilling and exciting journey, but it can also be a daunting task, filled with challenges and obstacles. However, with the right guidance and a solid plan in place, anyone can turn their cosmetic brand idea into a successful reality. That's why we're here, to help you every step of the way.

This comprehensive guide covers all the essentials you need to know to launch your cosmetics brand, from concept to launch. Whether you're an experienced entrepreneur, or just starting out, this guide will help you navigate the journey with confidence.

In the pages that follow, you'll find tips, strategies, and insights on how to create a winning brand, develop a product line, build a marketing plan, secure funding, and more. We'll share stories from real cosmetics entrepreneurs and experts, to help you understand what works, what doesn't, and how to overcome common challenges.

So, whether you're just starting to think about launching your own cosmetics brand, or you're already deep into the process, this guide is for you. We're here to support you and help you achieve your goals.

So, let's get started!

Preface

Starting your own cosmetics brand is an exciting and rewarding journey, but it can also be overwhelming. From developing your product concept to launching it to the market, there are countless details to consider and steps to take. That's where this guide comes in.

"Cosmetics Brand Launch: A Comprehensive Guide" is designed to walk you through every aspect of launching a cosmetics brand, from creating your product line to developing a marketing strategy to managing your finances. Whether you're a seasoned entrepreneur or just starting out, this guide will provide you with the information and resources you need to make your brand a success.

In this guide, you'll learn about the key factors that go into developing a product line, including market research, formulation, packaging, and labeling. You'll also discover how to build a strong brand identity, create an effective marketing plan, and navigate the challenges of manufacturing, distribution, and sales.

We've included practical advice, real-world examples, and case studies to help illustrate key concepts and provide you with a roadmap for success. And, because launching a cosmetics brand is a complex and multi-faceted process, we've included tips and tricks for staying organized and avoiding common pitfalls.

So, whether you're launching a brand out of passion or looking to grow your existing cosmetics business, this guide is the ultimate resource for getting started. So, let's get started!

Acknowledgements

Writing this guide on launching a cosmetics brand has been a rewarding and challenging experience, and I couldn't have done it without the support of many people.

First and foremost, I want to express my gratitude to my friends and family for their unwavering support and encouragement. Your belief in me means the world.

I would also like to extend a huge thank you to the cosmetic industry experts who generously shared their insights and experiences with me. Your input was invaluable in creating a comprehensive and useful guide.

I also want to thank the team at TR GROUP for providing me with the platform to share my knowledge and expertise. Your support and guidance have been instrumental in making this guide a reality.

Finally, I want to acknowledge the readers of this guide. Your interest in starting your own cosmetics brand and your willingness to learn is what inspired me to write this guide in the first place. I hope you find it helpful and informative as you embark on this exciting journey.

With heartfelt gratitude,

Tushar Raj

Prologue

Congratulations on taking the first step toward launching your own cosmetics brand! Starting a business is no small feat, and venturing into the beauty industry is even more exciting. With so many products, trends, and customer demands, it can be overwhelming to know where to start. That's why we've created this comprehensive guide, to help you navigate the process from concept to launch.

In this guide, we'll cover everything from conducting market research, developing your brand identity, creating product lines, securing funding, and launching your brand to the world. Whether you're a seasoned business owner or a first-time entrepreneur, our aim is to provide you with the knowledge and tools you need to succeed.

We understand that starting a cosmetics brand can seem like a daunting task, but with our help, we're confident that you'll be able to turn your dream into a reality. So, let's dive in and take this exciting journey together!

Author Info

Tushar Raj

CHAPTER ONE

Introduction

Welcome to "Cosmetics Brand Launch: A Comprehensive Guide"! This guide is designed to help you launch your own cosmetics brand, taking you step by step from the initial concept to the actual launch. Whether you're a seasoned entrepreneur or starting from scratch, this guide will provide you with the knowledge and resources you need to bring your brand to life.

A. Overview of the Guide

This guide covers all the key aspects of launching a cosmetics brand, from market research and product development to marketing and financial management. Each chapter is designed to be comprehensive, yet easy to follow, so that you can launch your brand with confidence.

B. Importance of a Comprehensive Guide

Starting a cosmetics brand can be a challenging and complex process, with many important decisions to be made along the way. This guide is designed to help you navigate the process, ensuring that you have the information you need to make informed decisions. Whether you're new to the cosmetics industry or have experience launching other brands, this guide will provide you with the tools you need to succeed.

C. Objectives of the Guide

The objective of this guide is to provide you with the knowledge and resources you need to launch your own cosmetics brand. Our goal is to help you:

1. Conduct thorough market research to understand your target audience and competition
2. Develop a strong brand identity that reflects your vision and values
3. Create a business plan and register your business
4. Develop high-quality cosmetics products that meet customer needs
5. Build a strong online presence and establish relationships with retailers
6. Launch a marketing campaign and build a customer base
7. Manage operations and logistics, including shipping and fulfillment
8. Track expenses and manage finances effectively

By the end of this guide, you will have the tools and knowledge you need to launch your cosmetics brand successfully. So let's get started!

CHAPTER TWO

Planning and Preparation

Welcome to the planning and preparation stage of launching your own cosmetics brand! This is a crucial step in creating a successful brand, so it's important to take your time and do it right.

A. Conducting Market Research

Before you start creating your brand and products, it's important to understand the market you're entering. Conducting market research will help you identify your target audience, understand their needs, and find out what they're looking for in a cosmetic brand. You can start by conducting online surveys, focus groups, and competitor analysis to gather data and information.

B. Identifying Your Target Audience

Once you've completed your market research, it's time to identify your target audience. Who are you creating your products for? What are their age, gender, and income range? What are their interests, hobbies, and lifestyles? Understanding your target audience will help you create products and marketing strategies that resonate with them.

C. Developing Your Brand Identity

Your brand identity is how your company is perceived by the public, and it's important to create a strong and consistent image. This includes developing your brand name, logo, slogan, and brand colors. Your brand should reflect the personality of your company and the values it stands for. It should also be unique and memorable, so that it stands out in a crowded market.

D. Creating a Business Plan

A business plan is a comprehensive guide that outlines your business goals, strategies, and financial projections. It's important to create a solid business plan before you start investing time and money into your brand. Your business plan should include a clear overview of your company, your target audience, your marketing strategies, your operational plans, and your financial projections.

E. Registering Your Business

Before you start selling your products, you'll need to register your business and obtain the necessary licenses and permits. This process may vary depending on your location and the type of business you're starting, so it's important to research the specific requirements for your area.

F. Sourcing Materials and Suppliers

Once you have your business plan in place, it's time to start sourcing materials and suppliers. You'll need to find suppliers who can provide you with high-quality raw materials and ingredients for your products, and you'll need to establish relationships with them. You may also need to find suppliers for packaging, labeling, and shipping materials.

That's it for the planning and preparation stage! You've done the hard work of researching your market, identifying your target audience, developing your brand, and creating your business plan. In the next chapter, we'll focus on product development. Stay tuned!

CHAPTER THREE

Product Development

Congratulations on making it this far! You have successfully conducted market research, identified your target audience, and developed your brand identity. Now it's time to get down to the nitty-gritty of product development.

Product development is a crucial step in launching your cosmetics brand. After all, the success of your brand will largely depend on the quality and appeal of your products. So, let's dive into the process of creating your products and getting them ready for launch.

A. Creating product prototypes

The first step in product development is to create prototypes of your products. This is a great opportunity to experiment with different ingredients, textures, and scents to see what works best. You can also get feedback from friends, family, and potential customers to see how they respond to your prototypes. Don't be afraid to make changes and tweaks until you're happy with the final product.

B. Testing and refining products

Once you have a solid prototype, it's time to test your product to ensure that it is safe, effective, and compliant with any relevant regulations. This includes conducting laboratory testing and clinical trials. You can also perform a patch test on a small group of volunteers to see how the product reacts to different skin types. Based on the results of your testing, you may need to make further changes to your product before moving forward.

C. Packaging design and production

Now that your product is ready, it's time to focus on packaging design. Your packaging should reflect your brand identity and appeal to your target audience. Think about the type of packaging that will work best for your product (e.g., pump bottles, jars, tubes, etc.). You'll also need to decide on the size, material, and labeling for your packaging. Once you have a design in mind, you can work with a manufacturer to produce your packaging.

D. Choosing a manufacturer

Finally, it's time to choose a manufacturer to produce your products. When selecting a manufacturer, consider factors such as cost, quality, speed, and reliability. You should also visit the manufacturer's facility to see their operations and make sure that they have the necessary certifications and equipment to produce your products. Once you have chosen a manufacturer, you can work with them to establish a production schedule and get your products ready for launch.

Product development can be a time-consuming and challenging process, but with patience, attention to detail, and a commitment to quality, you can create a product that you can be proud of. Good luck!

CHAPTER FOUR

Marketing and Sales

Congratulations, you've made it to the exciting part of launching your cosmetics brand - marketing and sales! At this point, you've developed your product line, established your brand identity, and set up your operations. Now it's time to get your products in front of the right people and start generating sales. In this chapter, we'll cover the essential elements of a successful marketing and sales strategy, including:

1. Building a strong online presence
2. Establishing relationships with retailers
3. Creating a sales strategy
4. Launching a marketing campaign
5. Building a customer base

Let's dive in!

1. Building a strong online presence:

Your online presence is critical to the success of your cosmetics brand. Consumers are increasingly turning to the internet to research and purchase products, so you need to make sure your brand is well-represented online. Here are a few key steps to take:

* Create a professional website: Your website is often the first point of contact between your brand and potential customers. It should reflect your brand identity and

provide all the information potential customers might need, such as product descriptions, pricing, and a contact form.

* Establish social media accounts: Social media is a powerful tool for reaching and engaging with potential customers. Choose the platforms where your target audience is most active and create profiles for your brand. Make sure to post regularly and share content that is relevant and interesting to your followers.

* Utilize influencer marketing: Partnering with influencers in your niche can be an effective way to reach a large and engaged audience. Work with influencers who align with your brand values and have a following that aligns with your target audience.

2. Establishing relationships with retailers:

Working with retailers can be a great way to get your products in front of a large number of potential customers. Here are a few tips for establishing successful relationships with retailers:

* Identify potential retailers: Research and make a list of retailers that align with your brand and target audience. Consider both online and brick-and-mortar stores.

* Reach out to retailers: Prepare a professional and informative pitch and reach out to potential retailers via email or phone. Make sure to highlight the unique features and benefits of your products, as well as your brand story.

* Negotiate favorable terms: Once you've established a relationship with a retailer, negotiate terms that are favorable for both parties. Consider factors such as pricing, payment terms, and marketing support.

3. Creating a sales strategy: Your sales strategy should outline how you plan to reach and convert potential customers into paying customers. Here are a few key

elements to consider:

* Set sales goals: Identify the sales targets you want to achieve, such as a certain number of units sold or a specific dollar amount in revenue.

* Determine your target customer: Clearly define who your target customer is, what their needs and wants are, and how your products meet those needs.

* Develop a sales plan: Create a detailed plan for how you will reach and convert potential customers into paying customers. This could include tactics such as email marketing, paid to advertise, or in-person events.

4. Launching a marketing campaign:

Your marketing campaign should be designed to raise awareness of your brand and drive sales. Here are a few tips for launching a successful marketing campaign:

* Determine your budget: Allocate a budget for your marketing efforts and prioritize the channels that are likely to be the most effective for reaching your target audience.

* Measure success: Make sure to track the results of your marketing efforts

E. Building a Customer Base

Building a customer base takes time and effort, but it is worth it in the end. Offer exceptional customer service, respond to customer inquiries and feedback, and continually evaluate and improve your products. Encourage your customers to share their experiences with others and to write reviews of your products. These actions will help you build a strong reputation and a loyal following.

In conclusion, building a customer base is a key component of success for any cosmetics brand. By focusing on creating a strong online presence, establishing relationships with retailers, developing a sales strategy, launching a marketing campaign, and providing excellent customer service, you will be well on your way to building a thriving business. Good luck!

CHAPTER FIVE

Operations and Logistics

As you embark on the journey of launching your cosmetics brand, it's crucial to have efficient operations and logistics in place. Having a well-oiled machine behind the scenes will help ensure your products are delivered to customers quickly and smoothly. In this chapter, we'll go over some of the key elements of operations and logistics that you should keep in mind.

1. Setting up an Efficient Supply Chain

Your supply chain is the backbone of your operations, so it's important to set it up properly from the start. To ensure that everything runs smoothly, consider working with a trusted third-party logistics (3PL) provider. They can handle everything from sourcing and procurement to shipping and fulfillment, freeing up your time and resources to focus on other important aspects of your business.

If you choose to manage your supply chain, make sure you have a robust system in place to track inventory, manage orders, and communicate with suppliers and manufacturers. You'll also want to make sure you have a clear understanding of the lead times and delivery schedules of each of your suppliers so that you can accurately predict when products will be available for sale.

2. Managing Inventory

Keeping track of your inventory is crucial to the success of your business. Overstocking can lead to cash flow problems, while understocking can result in stockouts and lost sales. To avoid these issues, consider using an inventory management system that will automatically track your stock levels and alert you when it's time to reorder.

In addition to managing your inventory levels, it's important to have a system in place for monitoring product quality. Regular checks and tests can help ensure that your products are consistent and meet your customers' expectations.

3. Shipping and Fulfillment

Once your products are ready to go, it's time to start shipping and fulfilling orders. To ensure that this process goes smoothly, it's important to have a clear and efficient shipping process in place. Consider partnering with a reliable shipping carrier, such as FedEx or UPS, and invest in good shipping software that will help you manage orders and track packages in real-time.

You should also make sure that you have a clear and concise return policy in place. Customers appreciate knowing what their options are if they're not satisfied with a product, and a clear return policy can help build trust and establish a good reputation for your brand.

4. Customer Service

Last but not least, it's essential to have a customer-centric approach to your operations. This means having a responsive and friendly customer service team in place to handle inquiries, answer questions, and resolve any issues that may arise. You can handle customer service in-house, or you can outsource it to a customer service provider. Either way, it's crucial to invest in the right tools and training to ensure that your customer service team is equipped to handle any situation that comes their way.

In conclusion, the operations and logistics behind your cosmetics brand are key to its success. By investing time and resources into setting up an efficient supply chain, managing your inventory, shipping and fulfilling orders, and providing excellent customer service, you'll be well on your way to creating a successful and sustainable cosmetics brand.

CHAPTER SIX

Financial Management

As you launch your cosmetics brand, it's important to keep a close eye on your finances. Having a solid understanding of your finances will help you make informed business decisions, track your progress, and plan for the future. In this chapter, we'll go over some of the key elements of financial management that you should keep in mind.

1. Budgeting and Forecasting

Before you start your cosmetics brand, it's important to create a budget that outlines your expected expenses and income. This will help you determine how much money you need to start your business and how much you need to generate in sales to break even. You should also create a sales forecast, which will give you an estimate of what you expect to sell in the coming months or years.

2. Tracking Expenses

Once your cosmetics brand is up and running, it's important to keep track of your expenses. This will help you understand where your money is going and identify areas where you can reduce costs. You should also keep track of your income and compare it to your budget to see how you're doing. If you find that your expenses are higher than expected or your sales are lower than anticipated, it's important to make adjustments to your budget and sales forecast to keep your business on track.

3. Bookkeeping

Good bookkeeping practices are essential to the success of your cosmetics brand. This means keeping accurate records of your income and expenses, as well as making sure that you're in compliance with all relevant tax laws. Consider hiring a bookkeeper or using accounting software to help manage your finances. This will free up your time and ensure that your financial records are accurate and up-to-date.

4. Seeking Investment or Funding

As your cosmetics brand grows, you may need to seek investment or funding to help it reach its full potential. This can come from a variety of sources, including venture capital firms, angel investors, or government grants. If you decide to seek investment or funding, it's important to have a clear and compelling pitch that highlights your brand's unique selling proposition and demonstrates its potential for growth.

In conclusion, financial management is an essential part of launching and running a successful cosmetics brand. By creating a budget, tracking expenses, keeping accurate records, and seeking investment or funding as needed, you'll be well on your way to creating a financially stable and thriving cosmetics brand.

CHAPTER SEVEN

Conclusion

Congratulations! You've made it to the end of our comprehensive guide to launching your own cosmetics brand. Launching a new business is no small feat, but with the right planning, preparation, and execution, you can make your vision a reality.

1. Reflection on the Launch Process

Take a moment to reflect on the journey you've been on so far. Think about the challenges you've faced and the lessons you've learned. Remember the highs and lows and all of the hard work that went into making your cosmetics brand a reality. Whether you're just starting out or you've been in business for a while, it's important to take time to reflect on your progress and celebrate your successes.

2. Final Thoughts and Advice

Starting a cosmetics brand is a journey that requires dedication, hard work, and a willingness to learn. There will be challenges along the way, but with a solid plan, a clear vision, and a focus on delivering high-quality products, you can turn your dream into a reality.

As you move forward with your cosmetics brand, remember to stay true to your vision and always put your customers first. Building a brand takes time and effort, but with persistence and determination, you'll be well on your way to creating a successful and sustainable cosmetics brand.

3. Future Growth and Expansion

Finally, as you continue to grow your cosmetics brand, keep an eye on the future. Consider ways to expand your product line, reach new customers, and grow your business. With a focus on innovation and customer satisfaction, the sky's the limit for your cosmetics brand!

In conclusion, launching a cosmetics brand is a thrilling and challenging journey, but with the right planning, preparation, and execution, you can make your vision a reality. Keep these final thoughts and advice in mind as you move forward and continue to grow your brand.

Printed by Libri Plureos GmbH in Hamburg,
Germany